She darted back to the ball and trapped it, but both fullbacks were on her again.

This time she got off a quick pass, right between the two.

Jacob was slicing to the goal. He took the ball out of the air with the inside of his knee.

He dropped the ball to the grass just as the goalie charged.

"Behind you!" Heidi yelled.

Books about the kids from Angel Park:

Angel Park All-Stars

Angel Park Soccer Stars

QUICK MOVES

By Dean Hughes

Illustrated by Dennis Lyall

Bullseye Books • Random House
New York

Library of Congress Cataloging-in-Publication Data
Hughes, Dean, 1943–
Quick moves / by Dean Hughes ; illustrated by Dennis Lyall.
p. cm. — (Angel Park soccer stars ; 8)
Summary: When she finds that she is no longer taller than most of
the other players, Heidi has to adjust to playing wing instead of striker.
ISBN 0-679-84358-2 (pbk.)
[1. Soccer—Fiction.] I. Lyall, Dennis, ill. II. Title.
III. Series: Hughes, Dean, 1943– Angel Park Soccer Stars ; 8.
PZ7.H87312Qu 1993 [Fic]—dc20 92-44933
RL: 4.5
First Bullseye Books edition: October 1993

Manufactured in the United States of America
10 9 8 7 6 5 4 3 2 1

New York, Toronto, London, Sydney, Auckland

for Jordan Snarr

★ 1 ★

Flying Low

Heidi Wells spun away from her defender and raced toward the goal.

Lian Jic, one of the Angel Park Pride midfielders, lifted a high pass toward her. Heidi saw her chance to head the ball into the net.

She ran hard and timed her jump just right.

She stretched her neck and reached with her head for the ball.

She was sure she had it.

But just then a big fullback from the Paseo Bandits flashed in front of her. He leaped higher and slammed the ball away.

The ball arched over the goal line and out of bounds. The chance for the goal was lost.

Heidi was mad.

The first half would soon be ending, and neither team had scored. The Bandits had a good team, but they had never been this tough to score on.

Heidi looked over at Lian. "Good pass," she yelled to him. "I thought I had it."

Lian walked over to her. "That's okay. That guy is just too tall for you."

Heidi didn't like that. She wanted to say, "Hey, I'm taller than *you* are."

Lian seemed to read her mind. "I could never play striker," he said. "I couldn't jump high enough."

What was that supposed to mean?

Heidi turned and walked away. But Lian had hit on something that Heidi didn't really want to think about. All during the spring season she had been having trouble getting up high enough to compete with the big fullbacks.

Jacob Scott took the corner kick. But a Bandit fullback got to the ball first and blasted it upfield.

Sterling Malone, Angel Park's best full-back, outran a couple of Bandits and took the ball back. He shot upfield with it and then passed off to Tammy Hill, one of the other girls in the starting lineup for the Pride.

The Pride was on the attack again.

Heidi dropped back toward the Bandits' goal. Then she trotted left of the goal area. Her defender followed.

The fullback who was covering her was a tall kid named Taylor Johnson. Heidi was faster, but Johnson didn't mind muscling her around when he got a chance. And that's what it took to keep her from getting open.

So Heidi let him think she was wearing down. She slowed to a walk and put her hands on her hips. She took a couple of deep breaths. She pushed her dark bangs off her sweaty forehead.

And she waited.

Johnson came up on her tight. He got between her and the goal.

A guy named Tim Thornburgh was playing midfield today, with Lian. He dribbled the ball up the middle, and then he slowed to a stop. He dropped the ball back to Adam Snarr, the sweeper.

The defense was set now. The Pride players were bogged down in the middle of the field.

Someone needed to make something happen.

But Heidi couldn't make her move yet. She drifted toward the middle of the field a little, still moving slowly.

She was still waiting for her chance.

Sterling suddenly darted up the field and Adam led him just right. Sterling took the pass and dribbled forward. Then he booted the ball over to Jacob Scott.

Jacob trapped the ball. He tried to dribble past a Bandit defender but got cut off.

Again, the Pride motion was stopped.

Coach Toscano yelled from the sidelines, "Come on, Jacob. Keep the ball moving. Let's go!"

Henry White, the Pride right wing, ran to Jacob and called, "Behind you."

Jacob turned and kicked the ball back to

Henry. Then he spun and shot toward the goal.

Henry saw the move and lifted a crossing pass toward the penalty box.

But the pass was off line. A Bandit fullback stepped in and stole the ball. He cleared the ball back up the field.

But Sterling outjumped a Bandit midfielder. He headed the ball back toward the Bandit goal.

Then he chased after the ball.

And Heidi finally saw her chance.

She burst away from her defender and angled through the goal area.

She was open and Sterling saw her.

He looped a pass in her direction.

Heidi had hoped for a low kick she could volley straight into the net. But the timing was right on the high pass. She leaped for a header.

The goalie had also seen what was coming. He dashed toward Heidi. He jumped high and reached over her head. And he grabbed the ball away just before Heidi could hit it.

But he couldn't pull the ball to his chest. He landed off-balance and crashed to the grass. As his shoulder hit the ground, the ball jarred loose.

Heidi took off after it. But she was too late.

Sterling was still coming hard. He got to the loose ball and slammed it at the goal.

The goalie was halfway to his feet as the ball sailed in his direction. He dove at the ball and got one hand on it.

But Sterling had *powered* the ball. It almost took the goalie's hand off.

And it *snapped* into the net.

Score!

Heidi spun around in time to see the ball hit the net.

"All right, Sterling!" she shouted. "Way to be there. Great shot."

Sterling waved his fists in the air. "Let's get some more now!" he yelled. Then he slapped hands with Heidi.

About then Jacob came flying in. He jumped right on Sterling's back. "Way to go! Way to go!" he was yelling. "It's about time we scored on these guys."

Heidi was yelling the same thing. She was happy that the Pride had finally taken the lead.

But she was also frustrated.

She had been within inches of that goal. That big goalie had reached right over the top of her.

But she couldn't worry about that now. The kickoff was coming, and the Pride needed to show the Bandits who the boss was.

That, however, was easier said than done.

Kyle Oshima, the Bandits' all-star forward, wasn't ready to back off and let the Pride run away with the match.

The guy was all over the place.

He made a good tackle and stole the ball from Miles Harris, who was playing fullback for Angel Park.

Miles was not a starter. He had come into the game for Tanya. He was a star basketball player, but he was new to soccer. And even though he was playing better all the time, Oshima was a tough guy to deal with.

Oshima knocked the ball past Miles and then chased after it. He controlled the ball and then dribbled straight at Billy Bacon, the stocky Pride fullback.

Billy came up close and tried to bang shoulders with Oshima.

But Oshima played it smart.

He bent forward and pressed his left shoulder against Billy. Then he flipped the ball behind his left foot. In the same motion, he spun off Billy's tackle.

Billy stumbled forward.

Oshima flashed back to the ball. He sliced toward the goal.

Nate Matheson, the Pride goalie, saw the move and yelled, "Tammy, cut him off!"

Tammy left her own man and broke toward Oshima.

Oshima let her come toward him. And then he kicked the ball back to . . .

But he didn't.

He only faked the pass.

But Tammy took the fake and tried to turn back. She slipped and fell to the grass.

Now Oshima had clear sailing to the goal.

He charged hard.

Nate ran straight at him.

But Oshima could cut on a dime. He suddenly broke to the right. Then he *lashed* the ball past Nate's feet.

The ball flew as if it had eyes. It got just past Nate's fingers—and slipped inside the goalpost!

And the match was tied.

Heidi had seen it all from a distance. She couldn't believe it. Oshima had gotten through the whole Pride defense—all by himself.

The guy was a great player. And he was getting better all the time. But Heidi could remember two years back—when she had made the all-star team, and Oshima hadn't.

The rest of the half was frantic. Both teams pushed hard to break the tie.

But neither team scored.

When Heidi walked off the field for half-time she was upset. She *knew* she could play better than she was playing.

★ 2 ★

A New Star

Nate came trotting up behind Heidi. "What's going on?" he said. "These guys shouldn't be that tough."

Heidi looked around at him. "Maybe they shouldn't be, but they *are*," she said.

"We're making them look better than they are," Nate told her. "We should have more goals by now."

"Go tell *them* we're supposed to win, Nate. I don't think anyone let them know yet."

"Someone needs to *show* them."

"Hey, don't look at me," Heidi barked at him. "I'm doing my best."

"I didn't mean that. I just—"

"You can be a real jerk sometimes, Nate."

Heidi turned and tromped off toward the water fountain. What right did Nate have to complain about the attack? He only stood in the goal and watched.

"The guy hasn't even worked up a sweat," Heidi mumbled to herself.

And yet, she knew she was making too big a deal out of the whole thing. Nate hadn't meant anything. He was her friend. What was wrong with her today?

The coach let all the players get a drink. Then he had them sit down together on the grass.

"I'm not sure what's happening," he told the players. "You don't seem to have much zip."

He stood and looked at them.

Coach Toscano usually sounded patient and polite as he spoke with his slight Brazilian accent. But he didn't sound very patient to Heidi right now.

"I think maybe you thought this match was going to be easy," he said.

Heidi ducked her head. The coach seemed to be looking straight at *her*.

But the coach said nothing to Heidi. He talked about shutting down Oshima in the second half.

"You can't let him go one-on-one with a fullback," Coach Toscano told his players. "That's what he loves to do. But if you stop him, you stop the Bandits. They play good defense, but they depend on one player to do their scoring."

The coach told Miles to stay in the match and to mark Oshima closely. "And the rest of you help Miles if Oshima gets anywhere close to shooting range."

"We've got to get our attack going too," Jacob said.

"That's right," the coach agreed. "And the attack looked best when Sterling worked his way forward. He makes things happen."

Heidi's head popped up.

"You midfielders drop back on defense if Sterling drives on through. But Sterling, go ahead and make a charge if you see the chance."

That was fine with Heidi.

She knew the coach believed in total soccer. He liked to get the fullbacks into the attack. And Sterling was the right guy to do the job. He was big and strong and fast.

Still, she and Jacob were the strikers. They had gotten the job done so far. Now the coach sounded as though he didn't believe in them.

But Heidi stopped herself. She was thinking wrong and she knew it. Sterling wasn't the problem.

Heidi just couldn't shake loose the memory of that Bandit goalie. The guy had reached *over her*. She had jumped as high as she could, but he had gotten higher.

How had he done that? No one had ever done that to her before.

And Johnson had outjumped her too. The memory left a sort of sick feeling in her stomach.

Heidi made up her mind to play the best second half of her life. She would make Johnson look like an idiot. And she would show that goalie who was the *boss*.

And so, when Heidi went back on the field, she worked hard. She watched for chances to get open for shots. And when she saw them, she left big Johnson standing in his tracks.

But the Bandits were still hanging tough on defense. The Pride players weren't getting the ball into shooting range.

Five minutes into the second half the score was still tied.

And then Lian and Henry worked a beautiful wall pass. Lian flipped the ball over to Henry and slipped past his defender. Henry shot the ball straight back to Lian— and Lian *streaked* up the right side of the field.

He drew two defenders over to cover him.

As Lian slowed, Henry ran past him. Lian shoved a little pass his way, and Henry took the ball in stride.

Henry charged down the touchline. Then he cut left.

Jacob was trying to work loose from his defender in front of the goal. Henry saw him and hit a pass in his direction.

Heidi saw what was happening and darted toward the goal.

But Jacob's defender beat him to the ball. Both boys kicked at the ball at the same time. The ball looped high in the air and over the end line.

The referee ran toward the boys. "Corner kick—blue team," he yelled.

Heidi was glad for the call. The Pride had some good plays that they used for corner kicks. This might be her chance.

Sterling, Henry, and Chris Baca, the left winger, lined up in front of the goal.

Heidi and Jacob took positions just outside the goal area. The plan was for Jacob to cut toward the goal as the ball was kicked. That would pull his defender with him.

Then Heidi would cut behind Jacob and use him as a screen to pick off her defender. If it worked, Heidi got open in the goal area, with the ball dropping toward her.

All she had to do was head the ball into the net.

If the pass was off line, the Pride still had four of their tallest players in position to go up for the header.

It was a play that had worked before. But Heidi had never wanted to make it work more than she did right now.

Lian got ready.

Heidi watched.

She stood still. She didn't look in the direction she was going to run. Johnson was leaning against her, trying to block her from making a move.

The big lug weighed a ton. Heidi felt like kicking his legs out from under him. But she waited and let him think he had her locked up.

Lian ran forward and lofted a good kick.

Jacob made his break.

Heidi waited for him to clear, and then—*bang*—she spun off Johnson and cut behind him.

Jacob's defender followed a couple of steps and then seemed to sense what was happening. He suddenly stopped.

Heidi was cutting hard. She ran into the guy, full force.

She bounced off as though she had hit a brick wall. She was on her backside when the ball came floating into the goal area.

The "brick wall" was waiting. He headed the ball out of danger.

And the chance was lost.

Heidi scrambled up, mad enough to punch the guy. But he was already running away. She had to get back into the action.

About a minute later the whistle blew as a Bandit hit the ball over the touchline.

Heidi stopped to take a breath or two, but then she heard the coach call out, "Sterling, you play forward for Heidi. Daniel, play fullback. Heidi, come off and rest for a minute."

Heidi looked up, stunned. "I don't *need* to rest," she yelled to the coach.

But he waved her over.

Heidi had *never* been pulled out of a tie match. The coach usually only took her out when the game was won.

What was this?

Heidi walked off the field. And the coach didn't say anything to her. He was too busy yelling to the players on the field.

Heidi stood and watched.

And for a time, nothing changed. The Bandits played a tough zone defense. They covered areas and switched off on different attackers. And they never let up.

The minutes were ticking away. Neither team could get much going.

But then a Bandit defender ran into Chris and knocked him down. The ref blew his whistle and gave Chris a free kick.

Chris got off a beauty. He hit the ball long, and Jacob made a great move to get to the ball first.

Jacob leaped in the air and cradled the ball with his middle. He let it drop to his feet. Then he quickly tapped it out to Henry, who came flying by at just the right instant.

Henry took the ball a few steps and then pulled up. And that's when his defender tried to stop too fast and slipped down.

Henry took the ball one step to his left and was clear. He kicked under the ball and looped a pass toward the goal.

Sterling *soared* into the air.

The goalie's only chance was to come out and jump with Sterling.

But Sterling was a mile high, and he used his head.

Like a club.

He *bashed* the ball into the goal.

The Pride had the lead, 2 to 1!

Heidi had run down the touchline as the play developed. And now she jumped into the air and cheered.

All the Angel Park players mobbed Sterling.

And Heidi loved it.

But she couldn't help thinking that the play would have been hers had she been on the field.

And she would have loved a chance to beat that goalie—the way Sterling had just done.

But she was still glad for the goal. And now the coach was saying, "Heidi, go back in at forward." And then he yelled, "Sterling, move back to fullback. I want you to cover Oshima."

That was great.

Heidi wanted to get back out there.

But what was the coach saying? Now that

scoring wasn't so important, it was okay to put Heidi back in at forward?

Was Sterling going to keep moving to the spot where the best player was needed?

Who was the star of this team anyway?

Replaced

Heidi told herself that the important thing, now, was to win the match. She had to quit worrying about everything else.

And so she went hard. She was rested, and she was a lot faster than any of the Bandit fullbacks anyway. She could get open any time she wanted to.

The problem was, the Angel Park players were not really pushing the attack. Only three or four minutes were left in the match. "Drop back," the coach kept yelling. "Clear the ball. That's it, use up time."

Heidi knew that's what they had to do. And she tried to help with the defense. But she still longed to get off a shot. One more goal would finish off the Bandits.

But it never happened.

Sterling led the defense. He used his power and quickness to harass the Bandit attackers. Miles was working hard too, and so was everyone else.

The defense was solid.

Oshima could hardly move without Sterling all over him. He usually couldn't get the ball. When he did, he was smothered.

And that's all it took.

The Pride didn't score again, but neither did the Bandits. The match ended 2 to 1.

When it was over, the Angel Park players told the Bandits they had played great—and they meant it. "You guys are going to win a lot of games if you play like that," Heidi heard Sterling tell Oshima.

Oshima shrugged. "I'd never score at all if I had you defending me every week."

Heidi thought that might be true. And she told herself she should be happy Sterling had come on so strong this spring. It meant the team would be all the better.

And, really, that's all that counted.

The more she thought that way the more she felt her bad mood lift.

"Hey," she told Nate and Jacob, "I know the mayor is planning to build statues of the three of us. But we might have to make room for Sterling too. He's getting *good*."

"I don't mind if he gets a statue," Jacob said. "But I think you three should be out in the desert somewhere. And I ought to be right in the center of Main Street."

"No. I want everyone together," Heidi said. "Pigeons like high places. They can land on Sterling's head—and leave me alone."

Maybe Heidi was still a little jealous. All the same, she was feeling good when the coach said, "Kids, come over here for a minute."

Everyone walked over to the coach, even a lot of the parents. "I'm really proud of you," Coach Toscano said. "The only bad news is that the Springers won again today. Because of the earthquake—and the shortened season—we only play each team once. I'm not sure anyone can beat the Springers."

"We can, Coach!" Billy called out. "They haven't played *us* yet. And we're not losing a game—*ever again!*"

Coach Toscano nodded and smiled. "Well, maybe. But the Bandits were tough today. I was just glad that when the chips were down, you kids showed you were ready to play."

Heidi knew that was true. And leaving the field for a couple of minutes was no big deal. Maybe the coach really had just wanted to let her catch her breath.

She never should have let herself get so upset.

And then the bomb dropped.

"We have a bye on Monday," the coach said. "That gives us a week to work on some things. I'm thinking we should make some lineup changes—to give us a little more power up front."

Heidi's breath caught.

The coach was looking straight at her. "Heidi, you used to be one of our tallest players, but a lot of the boys are growing really fast now. I'm thinking we can take better advantage of your speed if you play the wing."

Heidi stared at the coach. She tried not to let her face show what she was feeling. But inside, she was saying, "I'm a striker. A shooter. That's what I *do*."

"It's hard for you to get up high with some of these taller boys," the coach told her. "You got outjumped on a couple of headers today."

"That doesn't usually happen," Heidi said, sort of weakly.

"Well, the thing is, Heidi, you're a natural for the wing. You're quick, and you're a great passer."

"But I like playing in the middle."

"I know. But here's what I'm thinking. If we move Sterling up front, he'll make a big difference. He's got size, but he's also fast, and he's a good jumper. With you on the wing and him in the middle, we'll be stronger than ever."

"What about the defense?" Nate asked.

"That's just it," the coach said. "Up until now, I felt we had to have Sterling back on defense. But Miles is learning fast. He's got the speed to play sweeper for us. And Chris could move to fullback from wing."

Heidi tried to think what that would mean. Probably Tanya Gardner wouldn't be starting anymore. Was the coach giving up on the girls?

"Let's try it at practice. If it works, we'll use it against the Tornadoes next week."

So that was that.

The players all started to leave.

And Heidi heard Jacob congratulate Sterling.

Some friend!

Heidi walked away, heading for the parking lot with her parents. "That sounds like a good idea, Heidi," her father told her. "I think quickness is your real advantage. If you're not banging with those bigger guys, I think you'll do better."

"I thought I was doing okay before."

"Oh, you were. I didn't mean that, honey."

Heidi didn't listen to the rest. Her dad talked all the way back to the car about what a great idea this change was. Heidi felt like telling him to leave her alone.

But she said nothing.

She was almost to the car when Nate yelled, "Wait a sec, Heidi," and he came running over.

"You don't feel bad, do you?" he asked.

Heidi shrugged and tried to act as though it didn't matter much.

"Hey, I think it's a great idea. You'll be perfect at wing."

"I'm a forward."

"A wing *is* a forward."

"I'm a striker."

"I know. But you have to face it, Heidi. This will be the best position for you from now on."

Heidi knew she couldn't talk with Nate about this. She was getting angry all over again. "We'll see you later," she said. She got in the backseat of the car.

Her parents got in the front seat. And Heidi knew, as soon as she saw her dad turn around, that she was about to get another speech. "Hey, blockhead," he said, and he laughed.

Heidi stared out the window.

"I don't get this," Dad said. "The coach is

just putting you where you fit best. He's not saying you aren't any good."

"I know that," Heidi said.

"When I was a kid, I played center in basketball—until I got into high school. By then I wasn't big enough, and I played forward after that. What's the big deal?"

"Who said it was a big deal?" Heidi said. She tried to sound casual about the whole thing.

But now Mom had turned around too. "Honey, you must have known that the boys would grow bigger than you someday."

Sure, Heidi had thought about it, but it had always seemed something in the distant future. Like high school. It hadn't seemed anything she would have to deal with right away.

"Look, Heidi," Dad said. "It's lucky you like soccer so much. In basketball, size means a lot more. The great soccer players are usually not that big. You'll just be able to use your skills better on the wing."

"A lot of strikers aren't tall, Dad. I can play against any *boy!* I don't care how big he is." Heidi had stopped trying to hide her anger.

"Okay. Okay," Dad said. He ducked, as though she were about to punch him in the back of the head. "But where will you play your very best? The coach thinks it's on the wing. And I think he's right."

"I'm just as good as Sterling," Heidi shot back. "Why does he get *my* position?"

Mom took over. "It's not who is better," she said. "It's where you each fit best on the team."

Heidi didn't listen anymore. This whole thing wasn't fair—no matter what anybody said.

★ **4** ★

Winged

So Sterling was the new striker.

When he made mistakes, that didn't seem to matter. The coach just worked with him.

Heidi did everything she could to show who the better player was. All that seemed to do, however, was prove to the coach that he was right about her playing the wing.

Jacob and Nate kept telling Heidi what a great idea the change was.

Heidi thanked them, very nicely—and then told herself she'd like to break their legs.

On Monday the Pride got great news. The Springers had lost! That meant the Pride and the Springers were tied with the Kickers for first place—each with one loss.

And more good news came on Thursday, just before the Angel Park players were about to start their match.

The Springers beat the Kickers, and now the Pride had a chance to go all the way. They had to beat the Tornadoes today, and then beat the Springers for the championship.

That was the good news.

The bad news was, the Springers' loss had been to the Tornadoes. That meant the Tornadoes had to be *tough*.

The Tornadoes had beaten both the Kickers and the Springers. They had gotten off to a bad start, with two early losses, but they were really rolling now.

Heidi made up her mind to be a team player. She wasn't going to let her team down now. The match was too important.

That's what she told herself.

But when the action started, everything felt wrong. She couldn't seem to get into the action. Maybe some of it was just her attitude about the position. She knew that, but she couldn't seem to push herself to do any more than she was doing.

The Tornadoes had some great players. Hugh Roberts thought he was better than he was—but he was very good. And Rockwell, the kid everyone called "Rocket," seemed faster than ever.

If the Tornadoes had a weakness, it was that they sometimes thought too much about their attack, and they got loose on defense.

Early in the match, that's exactly what happened. The Pride had plenty of chances to score.

But no one could get the ball in the goal! Maybe Sterling was too nervous.

He got off two shots that really should have gone in. Both times, however, he tried to kick the ball too hard. He blasted some real *missiles*.

But he got under the ball and sent both shots flying over the crossbar.

Jacob messed up too. He had a chance to drive in a header, off a great pass by Henry. But he mistimed his jump. The ball grazed off the top of his head and right into the goalie's arms.

At least the Tornadoes weren't getting close to the Pride goal.

Or at least not at first.

And then Miles made a big mistake.

Rockwell was a rocket all right, but so was Miles. And the two were really flying at each other. Rockwell just couldn't shake Miles loose.

But then Roberts made a great move with the ball and broke through the middle of the field.

When Adam cut him off, Roberts stopped. Then he broke ahead again.

Adam stayed tough. He moved in for a tackle, and he was able to kick the ball away.

But Roberts ran after it. He tried to crowd Adam aside with his shoulder. Somehow their legs tangled and both went down.

No whistle.

For a moment Heidi thought that Billy was going to get to the ball. But Rocket came blasting in.

He slowed and took control of the ball. Then he spun to keep Billy from tackling.

With his back to Billy, he gave a feint to

the left. Then he twisted and was *gone* to the right.

But Miles was right there. He ran with Rocket and cut off his angle to the goal.

Rocket slowed and looked to pass.

And then blasted away again.

Miles was beaten. He tried to step back and keep his position. But he only tripped Rocket.

The whistle did sound this time.

The foul was in the penalty box. That meant a penalty shot.

Rocket was an experienced player. He knew what to do.

Nate would have to gamble and dive one direction or the other. Rocket ran at the ball and looked left as he *hammered* the ball right.

Nate had followed Rockwell's eyes.

He dove the wrong way as the ball hit the net behind him.

And the Tornadoes had the lead!

Heidi had watched it all.

In fact, she felt that was all she was doing today—watching.

She always seemed out of the action, away

from the goal area. She just couldn't get into the flow of things.

As she walked up the field to get ready for the kickoff, she heard her father yell, "Come on, Heidi. Make something happen. You're floating around out there. Go after those guys."

Heidi couldn't believe it. She was playing her new position. Couldn't he understand that?

But then the coach shouted, "Heidi, go after that big fullback. He can't cover you. You act like you don't want to play."

Heidi didn't look at the coach—or her father.

She stomped over to her position and got ready for the kickoff. Heidi was sure she was doing everything she could—from where she had to play now. Why was everyone getting on *her* back?

Sterling and Jacob were the guys missing the shots!

After the kickoff, the teams battled in the middle of the field for a time. The ball kept going back and forth, and no one could make much of a move.

And then Heidi got a chance to do something. She picked up a bad pass and broke down the touchline. She outran her defender and angled toward the goal.

She saw Jacob running down the middle of the field. She lobbed him a center pass. But she hit the ball too hard. It sailed well over Jacob's head.

The Tornado goalie ran out and grabbed the ball. Then he punted it up the field.

Heidi hated these long center passes. It wasn't something she had had to do before. And she wasn't good at it.

Chris would have gotten the ball to Jacob—and they might have scored.

Or . . . he might have gotten the ball to Heidi. And *she* might have scored.

But she wasn't supposed to think that way. Everyone had already told her that.

Lian took the ball away from a Tornado player. The Pride was coming back on attack.

Heidi stayed wide even though she wanted to work her way closer to the goal area.

Lian hit a perfect pass to Tammy. Tammy took the ball toward the touchline and looked for an opening.

The Tornadoes were clogging things up pretty well. So Tammy dropped back and left the ball for Miles.

Miles moved to his right. He dribbled the ball ahead. Then suddenly he cut to the left.

He beat his defender and shot a pass upfield.

But he had blasted the ball ahead without aiming at any one player. The ball was rolling down the center with several players after it.

Rocket was the first to get to it. He tried to kick the ball over to his wing, but Heidi darted in and stole it. She turned and tried to hit a quick pass ahead to Jacob.

Rocket got back quickly and cut between Heidi and Jacob. He was about to block the ball with his body. But he got his arm up, and the ball hit him in the hand.

The whistle sounded and Heidi got a free kick.

She set the ball down. She looked ahead to see where her teammates were. She stepped hard at the ball and faked a long pass. Then she nudged the ball off to Lian.

Rockwell had taken Heidi's fake and dropped back a little. Lian had room to make a run with the ball.

He charged ahead until Rocket made a move back toward him. Then Lian kicked a long pass up the field.

Henry took the ball on the right side. Then he broke toward the center.

Sterling made a great move. He suddenly turned on his speed and shot behind his defender—straight toward the goal.

Henry blasted a perfect center pass at Sterling.

And Sterling went flying.

He got way up above the charging goalie, and he got his head on the ball.

He lashed it hard.

And high.

The ball sailed above the crossbar and missed the goal again.

He came down kicking at the grass. "Oh, man!" he shouted. "How did I miss that?"

Heidi trotted over to him. "You're trying to put too much power on your shots," she said. "Just relax."

"You ought to be playing forward," he said. "I feel all wrong up here."

"You'll be all right," Heidi said. And she did know he could learn the position—in time. But what if they lost the match while he was trying to learn?

And that's what everyone must have been thinking as the players walked off the field at halftime.

The Pride had not gotten a goal. The score was still 1 to 0. If something didn't happen soon, Angel Park was in trouble.

Heidi was almost sure that the coach would put everyone back to their normal positions for the second half. And then maybe she could show a few people what a forward was supposed to do.

Maybe that was the wrong way to think—

according to her parents and the coach. But the team needed someone to step in and save the day.

And Heidi was more than willing to do it.

★5★

Making Moves

Coach Toscano gave his usual talk to the kids. They were doing well. They needed to pick up the pressure on the attack a little and everything would be all right.

What?

Heidi couldn't believe this.

The Pride hadn't scored. The team was in danger of getting knocked out of the championship.

And the coach thought everything was just fine?

"Coach, maybe I ought to go back to my regular position for the rest of the match," Sterling said.

Now *there* was an idea.

"I've thought about that," the coach said. "But our attack looked good. We just didn't get the ball in the goal. And our defense looked great. We haven't lost anything there. Let's just stick with what we're doing. We'll be all right."

Heidi was staring at the man.

Nate leaned over and told her, "He's right, Heidi. Sterling looked good. We'll get some goals. We'll win."

Now Heidi was staring at Nate.

"But you have to get into the attack more. You look like you're just hanging around, waiting for something to happen."

"Nate."

"Yeah?"

"Take a sniff of your socks. You need something to wake you up."

"We're going to win, Heidi. You watch."

Heidi got up. She hoped Nate was right.

But she wished the coach would get scared before long and decide to put her back where she *belonged*.

But that's not what happened.

The second half started much the way the first half had. The teams battled back and forth with no score. And yet, the Pride kept coming close.

This time it was Lian who missed on a shot he normally would make. Maybe everyone was starting to strain a little too hard.

But then Henry ran after a ball that seemed headed across the touchline. He stopped it just before it got to the line. Then he turned and looked out across the field.

He kicked the ball toward the middle of the field, probably shooting for Tammy. Rocket dashed in first and trapped the ball. And then he bolted ahead with the ball.

He dribbled toward Miles, and Miles got ready.

It was speed against speed.

But Rocket slowed and stepped over the ball with his right foot. He faked a little push with his left.

But the ball was gone!

Miles had kept his eye on the ball and hadn't taken the fake. He kicked the ball free. Then he beat Rocket to it.

Miles slapped a quick pass over to Tim. Tim controlled the ball and took a look upfield. Chris was breaking toward him. Tim shot him a good, low pass.

Chris dribbled once, twice, and then lifted a long pass down the left touchline.

Suddenly Heidi realized that she should have darted to the ball. But she was unsure of herself, and she had waited too long.

Lian was the one who chased after the ball. He got a pass off toward Jacob, but Lian was well marked. The pass was off line.

Jacob ran hard. He beat Rocket to the ball.

He dribbled across the field, but the Tornado defense was dropping back fast. The early chance for a shot was lost.

Heidi was mad at herself. If she had made her move at the right time, she could have kept the ball moving toward the goal.

But now she waited again.

She didn't want to break to the middle and clog things up. She was never sure what to do from this new position.

She realized that Jacob needed help. But she made her move too late. She ran toward the goal, but the defense was stacked in tight.

And that's when a fullback doubled Jacob from behind and took the ball away. The girl spun and kicked the ball upfield, clearing it away from her goal.

But Daniel Lakey was there, playing midfield for the Pride. He knocked the ball down with his chest. Then he kicked it back toward the goal.

Jacob made a great move.

He ran at the ball, ahead of Roberts. He controlled it with the inside of his foot, and he whipped it straight past Roberts's feet. Then he charged past Roberts and chased the ball down.

He reached the ball with open space in front of him. And he saw Sterling near the goal area.

Sterling was covered by two big fullbacks, but Jacob kicked under the ball and arched it toward the goal.

Sterling broke to the ball.

So did both defenders.

But Sterling outjumped the other two. He got way up and timed his jump just right. Then he gave the ball a shove with his head.

This time he didn't slam it too hard. He saw the open net on the left side, and he aimed his shot perfectly.

The ball flopped into the net.

The Pride had finally scored!

The Angel Park players didn't really go nuts. They seemed to be relieved, more than anything. And besides, they still had work to do.

"Now we're on our way!" Jacob told Sterling. "That was a *great* header. I can't believe how high you jumped."

"Good shot, Sterling," Heidi said.

She was really happy.

Fairly happy.

At least she *wanted* to be happy. She knew she *should* be happy.

And she did want to win the match. But she had still been holding out hope that the coach might send her back to her old position. No chance of that now.

"Hey, it's still only tied," Sterling was telling everyone. "We need to get some more goals. Let's *rip* these guys now."

Heidi saw Rocket and Roberts talking. They didn't like that idea one bit. Heidi knew they weren't going to give up without a good fight.

And she was ready to give it to them.

But she could hear her dad again. "Heidi,

get in there and *play*. You're still hanging back."

Heidi was sure her dad didn't know what he was talking about. She felt like telling him so. But she kept her mind on the match.

The Tornadoes came at the Pride hard.

Rocket faked Miles again. And this time Miles gambled and lost. Rocket got by him and then drove a hard shot at the goal.

Nate took a quick step to his left and dove. He was stretched out all the way when he caught the ball.

But he got it!

And then he jumped up and punted the ball out to Henry. Henry took the ball back the other way.

Heidi knew that Nate had made a great save. She was frightened to think the Pride could still lose this match.

She made up her mind to do something about that.

She stayed wide on the wing for now. She watched as Henry got the ball over to Daniel, and then as Daniel kicked it to Tammy.

Heidi broke away from her defender and ran to open space. She yelled, "Tammy, here!" Tammy shot a pass in her direction.

Heidi had to slow and come back to the ball. A defender moved in on her.

But she rushed ahead and beat the defender. And she raced down the middle of the field.

She charged toward the goal until she pulled in two defenders. Then she kicked the ball to Jacob.

She tried to get open for a return pass, but Jacob got trapped between two defenders. He couldn't get rid of the ball.

One of the defenders kicked the ball away. It bounced toward Tammy, and she saw Heidi coming hard.

Tammy hit the ball to Heidi, and Heidi made another run at the goal. This time she got picked up by a defender and forced back outside, toward the wing.

But she pulled up and let her defender slip by. Then she hit a center pass toward the front of the goal area.

Jacob had moved back, and he tried to go up for a header. But he was covered well.

The defender got his head on the ball, but he couldn't get much power into it. The ball bounced free in front of the goal area.

And Sterling was there.

He knocked the ball down with the inside of his foot. Then he spun and fired. It was a long shot, but it was a bullet.

The goalie reacted an instant too late. The ball whizzed just past his fingertips.

Zip!

It caught the net.

The Pride had taken the lead, 2 to 1.

And Sterling got mobbed.

Heidi was happy. She was glad she had gotten in the act and helped get the ball into shooting range. She was especially glad to be ahead in the match, finally.

But she didn't celebrate as wildly as she normally did.

Sterling got his third goal of the day just before the end of the match. Heidi didn't have much to say that time either.

When the match was all over, the Pride players went crazy. "Great comeback!" the coach was shouting.

And it was.

Heidi told herself she was very pleased.

But she just wanted to go home.

★ 6 ★

Friends?

Heidi listened to the coach's little speech. "I'm really pleased with our new lineup," he told the kids. "I'm glad we stuck with it. We have the right combination now to beat the Springers and win the championship."

Heidi was pretty sure that was an insult—no matter what everyone had been telling her.

As soon as the coach finished, Heidi got up, grabbed her sports bag and headed for the parking lot.

"Heidi, wait up," Nate called to her.

Nate and Jacob both hurried to catch up.

Heidi didn't want this. "I've got to go," she said. "My parents are waiting for me."

The truth was, her parents were talking

to some other parents. They hadn't even started walking toward the car yet. But Nate didn't say that.

"See, I told you. Toward the end, you were getting a feel for the wing." Nate had been wearing a sweatband over his blond hair. He pulled it off now. "And Sterling is going to be a *great* striker."

"Yup. You're right. Everything is wonderful. See you later." She started to walk away again.

"Heidi, you're acting like a spoiled brat."

Heidi spun around. "What?"

"You heard me."

"No. I don't think I did, Nate. A *friend* wouldn't call me something like that. I must have heard wrong."

She was off again. But Nate and Jacob ran after her. They got on opposite sides of her and walked the same speed she was walking. Fast.

"He didn't mean it . . . in a bad way," Jacob said.

"You're right, Jacob. 'Spoiled brat,' to Nate, is probably a compliment. After all, Nate gets CD players for Christmas and trips to Europe for summer vacation."

"I'm not spoiled," Nate said, smiling. "I'm really nice—for a rich kid."

That didn't go over so well. Nate was trying to get Heidi to laugh—and maybe ease up a little.

But she let out a huffy, long breath, and kept right on walking.

"Okay," Nate said. " 'Spoiled brat' was a poor choice of words. I just mean—"

"You just mean that you're glad Sterling —your *hero*—is getting the goals while I watch from the sidelines."

But Heidi knew she had admitted more than she wanted to.

"See. *That's* what I'm saying. You're afraid you won't score as many goals. You're jealous."

"*I am not.*" Heidi had come to a stop. She pointed a finger at Nate's nose. "I *liked* playing striker. That's my position. I don't want to change to another one."

"I'd change from goalie if it would help the team."

"You would not."

"Yes, I would. I'll play any position I can play best. And that's what you should do. We can win the championship next week if you'll quit worrying about yourself and play for the *team.*"

Heidi was furious, but she didn't say anything. She couldn't believe what a jerk Nate was being.

The thing that made her most angry was that he was right!

Heidi knew that. But it didn't make things any easier. She couldn't help what she was feeling.

Nate was supposed to be her friend. Why couldn't he forget about being right for a minute and just try to understand?

"Heidi," Jacob said, "being a wing isn't that different. It's just another kind of forward. You'll still get goals."

"She will if she *plays,*" Nate said. "I don't know what she was doing today. I think she was trying to make the team look bad so the coach wouldn't like the new lineup."

"*Nate!*" Heidi shouted. "You don't know what you're talking about. Leave me alone. I don't ever want to talk to you again."

And Heidi walked away one more time. But this time the boys didn't follow.

Heidi marched up to the car and tried to open the door, but it was locked.

She was left waiting until her parents finally showed up. Then she had to listen to some more nice speeches. The new lineup was great. Sterling was *wonderful*. Heidi just had to get into the action a little more.

Heidi said *nothing*. She breathed very hard, though. That was her way of saying, "I'm angry, folks, so leave me alone."

But they didn't seem to get the hint.

So Heidi went home to her room. She punched her pillow a few times. Then she sat down on the floor.

"No one understands," she said out loud.

But the truth was, everything that jerk Nate had said was true. He was just a jerk for saying it.

The phone rang. A few seconds later, Heidi heard her mom shout, "Heidi. Telephone."

"I'm busy," she muttered to herself. But she got up. She walked to the family room and picked up the phone.

"Yeah?"

"Heidi, don't hang up, okay?"

Heidi almost did. But it wasn't the really *big* jerk. It was just the medium-sized one—Jacob.

"I need to talk to you for a minute. Okay?"

"So talk."

"Are you still mad?"

"What do you mean 'still mad'? I just barely *got* mad. I plan to *be* mad for at least a couple of years."

Jacob laughed.

And then, so did Heidi. Why did she have to be funny even when she didn't want to be?

"How come you got so upset? All Nate was saying—"

"I know what he was saying."

"Don't you think he's right?"

"What does that have to do with it?"

Jacob was thrown off track a little. "Well . . . do you think he *was* right?"

"He was right about what he said. But he was still wrong."

"Oh."

Heidi didn't know what that meant either, but she was still in a cranky mood.

"So you don't want to play wing—even if it is a good position for you?"

That was putting it bluntly, but it did sum things up.

And yet it didn't at all.

Something about the whole conversation was wrong.

"Jacob, you really wouldn't understand, okay? And I don't want to talk about it."

"Maybe I do understand."

"I don't think so, Jacob."

Jacob hesitated, but then he said, "Well, maybe. But I remember when I started playing baseball, and I was about the smallest kid on the team."

"So what?"

"I don't know. I just know how it felt. Sixth graders seemed like giants, and they were smashing home runs and everything."

"Jacob, I think your mind is wandering. What does any of that have to do with me?"

"Heidi, just listen for a sec." He took a couple of heavy breaths himself. "Kenny was my same age, but he was a lot bigger. He was hitting home runs when he was in third grade. It seemed like it wasn't fair."

Heidi was starting to make the connection, but she didn't like it. "I can play soccer as well as *anybody* on the team, Jacob. You don't have to feel sorry for me."

"That's not what I'm saying."

"Then what *are* you saying?"

"Well, it seems sort of unfair that you used to be one of the tallest players, and now, everyone is growing bigger. So you have to lose your position. And it's not your fault."

"Jacob, that's not . . ."

Wait a minute. That *was* it.

Heidi didn't know what to say.

"When I started playing soccer you were taller than I was," Jacob said. "Now I'm taller than you—and I get to play striker. But Sterling gets to take *your* position. It's kind of a rotten deal. Because you can't do anything about it."

"That's right," Heidi said, and then she admitted the fear she had been feeling all week. "Jacob, when I was nine or ten, I was as good as *any* boy. I thought I always would be. Now I'm afraid the boys are all going to be better than I am."

"No way, Heidi. You're quick. And you have all the skills. You can be the best wing in the league—not just this year but when we get older, too."

"Do you really think so?"

"Sure. I may be taller than you, but you're

five times the soccer player I am. You always will be."

Heidi was surprised Jacob would say that. And embarrassed. She couldn't think what to say.

Finally she snarled, "Yeah, and don't you forget it!"

"Don't worry. I won't." Jacob pretended to be frightened.

A long pause followed. Heidi was thinking. She knew there was one thing she needed to say. But it wasn't easy.

"Uh . . . well—anyway—thanks, Jacob."

"Sure."

"I'll see you at practice."

"Okay."

"And Jacob?"

"Yeah?"

"Let's beat the Springers on Monday."

"Good idea. Are you going to feel okay about playing wing?"

"No." Heidi thought for a time and then added, "But I'm going to be the best one in the league."

"Now you're talking," Jacob said. "Let's win the championship."

Heidi thought that was a pretty good idea.

7

Winging Along

═══════════════════════════════

After school the next day the Pride held practice. The players who were on the Angel Park baseball team—including Jacob—showed up barely in time. But Nate and Heidi had gotten to the park early.

They did their stretches with the other players.

But Heidi didn't talk to him. Nate hadn't even bothered to call the way Jacob had.

Coach Toscano talked to the kids before he started any drills. "The Springers didn't play well against the Tornadoes—and they got beat. But they *hammered* the Kickers. And they think they're going to do the same thing to us."

Nate said, "We can't let them do that."

"Let's just play together as a team—the way we did in the second half yesterday," Coach Toscano said. "If we do that, no one can beat us."

Heidi raised her hand.

"Yes, Heidi?"

"I think this new lineup is good," she said. "I'm getting the hang of playing wing. And Sterling is going to be a *great* striker."

"That's exactly right," the coach said. "We've struggled with a couple of teams that aren't really that good. But we finally got it going yesterday. I think the Springers are going to be surprised."

Heidi nodded and said, "That's right."

But she could feel Nate was staring at her.

And as soon as the coach told the kids to line up for some dribbling drills, Nate walked over.

"That's exactly what *I* said—and you got mad at me for it."

"It isn't the same."

"It is too. Almost word for word."

"Okay, maybe you *said* the same thing, but you said it . . . different. You're still a jerk."

"Different? What do you mean *different?*"

But the coach called out, "Heidi. Nate. Line up."

So they lined up.

Nate was still mumbling something about Heidi being off her rocker. Heidi acted as though she didn't hear him. The guy really was a jerk.

Soccer mattered so much to Nate—and winning—that sometimes he forgot about everything else. Why couldn't the guy be a little more like Jacob? Why couldn't he have stopped to think what Heidi was feeling when she lost her position?

But for the moment, Heidi was more concerned about learning her position than arguing with Nate. When the coach had the kids do some five-on-five attack drills, Heidi kept asking questions.

"Don't worry that much whether you're a wing or a striker," the coach told her. "This is total soccer. When you get an opening, go for the goal."

"Won't I crowd things in the middle?"

"You can. So you have to learn when to make a move and when not to. But you're both forwards, and it's important that you not hang back when the action moves to the goal."

Heidi tried it that way. Her attack team brought the ball toward the goal. She started wide, keeping her defender with her.

But then Jacob took a pass from Henry on the right side of the goal area.

Heidi broke toward him.

She sliced across the goal area toward the penalty box. Jacob tried to scoot a pass to her.

Nate bolted forward and dove on the ball, but the play was close. Another step and Heidi would have slammed the ball into the net.

"That's the idea," the coach called out. "You timed that just about right. When you see the chance, go for it."

"Good move, Heidi," Nate told her.

"Oh, thanks so much, Nate," Heidi told him. She gave him a super sweet smile. "Coming from you, a compliment means *so much.*"

Nate rolled his eyes and turned away.

Heidi knew who was being a jerk now. But she couldn't stop herself.

At least practice kept going well. And Heidi was feeling more involved in the attack all the time.

When practice was over, Heidi changed her shoes and then got her bike. She was sort of expecting Nate to say something to her—maybe even try to patch up their quarrel.

In fact, she was sort of hoping.

But he didn't.

She found herself taking her time. It crossed her mind that Jacob might try to bring Nate over, if Nate wouldn't come on his own.

But he didn't.

And so she got on her bike and started pumping away.

And then she slammed on her brakes and put one foot down.

She wasn't going to let this happen. She was still sort of mad at Nate, but the two of them had been friends for a long time. She had to get this whole thing straightened out.

She looked back and saw Nate and Jacob, talking, not yet riding away on their own bikes. She dropped her bicycle and walked back to them.

"Sooooo . . . it sure has been nice weather lately," she said. "But then again, it could rain. What do you guys think?"

She grinned.

"It's been kind of hot, if you ask me," Nate said.

"Well, yes. But then, it can get that way around here—this time of year."

All three were smiling, but no one seemed ready to say *it*.

"I'm sorry you were such a jerk to me," Heidi finally said.

"Jerk? Why was *I* a jerk? All I said was that you'd be a good wing."

"*Jacob* is more *understanding* than you are."

"Oh, really? So what is it he understands that I don't?"

"He's been short. You never have been."

"What are you talking about? I used to be twenty-one inches tall."

"When?"

"When I was born."

"Hey, that's *tall* for a new baby."

"Oh." Nate thought for a moment. "Hey, why do I have to be short to understand *you*? You've always been tall, too."

"It's way too complicated for you to understand, Nate."

"I'll try to explain it to him," Jacob said.

"Okay." Heidi turned and walked back toward her bike.

But halfway there, Nate said, "Heidi, you're still our best player. Sterling is doing well, but he can't do all the stuff you can do."

"Uh-huh. Sure."

"I'm serious, Heidi."

"I'm not as good as you."

"Yeah, you are. I think I'm probably the best goalie in the league. You're the best forward."

"Wing."

"That's still a forward."

Heidi thought for a moment. She was sort of embarrassed.

"Well, you're still a jerk," she finally said. "But you're a good judge of soccer players."

Heidi picked up her bike and got on. She

circled back toward the boys, and as she whizzed by them, she said, "Thanks. But you're still a jerk."

And she was gone.

She didn't want to say something like that to Nate and look at him at the same time.

That evening everyone in Heidi's family had something different to do. Dad was the only one home, and he was outside fixing up some of the damage the earthquake had done to their driveway. Dinner was "grab your own—there's sandwich stuff in the refrigerator."

Heidi had a little homework to do, but it was Friday, and she didn't feel like getting around to it yet. So after she ate, she turned the TV on and started switching channels, trying to find something she liked—like, say, a "Mr. Ed" rerun.

Her dad came in when she was checking out an old movie. It was one of those tap-dancing World War II films. Heidi sort of liked those—or at least the dancing parts.

Dad said he had to run to a hardware store, but he stopped long enough to say, "So how did practice go tonight?"

"Great."

"Are you still upset about playing wing?"

"Why would I be upset? Wing is a good position."

"That's right, Heidi. I hope you're serious about that. Is it really all right with you if Sterling takes your position?"

"Why would I care about that, Dad? Don't be so thickheaded. Sterling's perfect for the job."

Heidi switched channels. The tap-dancing had ended and the war was returning.

"I'm serious, Heidi. I think the wing is where you really should be playing."

"Dad, that's what I've been trying to tell you. Aren't you listening?"

Dad rolled his eyes—the way Nate had done at practice. "Well, I'm glad we had this little talk," he said. "I think I finally have you straightened out."

"Yeah. Thanks, Dad. We need to have these chats more often. I always listen to everything you tell me."

Dad rolled his eyes one more time.

And then he left.

8

Making Something Happen

Heidi felt great when she showed up for the big match. She had made up her mind to forget all the other stuff and just play her best. She really wanted to win the championship, and she was sure the Pride could do it.

And then she spotted Robbie Jackson and Peter Metzger—and all the rest of the Springers.

The Springers were *tough*.

They had always had a good team, but this year a new kid was playing for them. He was a guy named Aly Sarr. He had moved to Angel Park from Senegal, in

Africa. He spoke mostly French, and he played mostly *fantastic*.

Heidi had watched him play against the Gila Monsters. The Springers had won, 7 to 0, and Aly had scored five of the goals. He wasn't as fast as Rocket Rockwell, but he had more moves than any kid Heidi had ever seen.

Before the match started, while all the players were stretching, Nate came over to talk to Heidi. "Jacob told me what you guys talked about on the phone," he said.

Heidi waited. Finally she said, "Yeah? What about it?"

She was still just a little irritated with Nate. "Well, I never really thought about it that way."

"Yeah?"

"Well . . . I'm sorry."

"So do you know why you were a jerk?" Heidi asked, and now she was finally smiling.

Nate thought about it for a few seconds. "Well, one thing I told you isn't really true. If someone took my position away, I wouldn't just say, 'Oh, great. That's good for the team.' It was kind of stupid of me to tell you that."

Heidi nodded, and she flashed her big smile, with the deep dimples. "I'm sure glad you figured that out," she said. "Now let's forget it and win this match."

Nate agreed.

While Heidi continued to do her stretches, she heard Coach Toscano talking to Miles. "You're going to have your hands full with that new kid," he said. "Just don't gamble and take his fakes. Keep your eyes on the ball."

"Don't worry. I can deal with him," Miles said.

Miles was always confident. And that was good—up to a point.

But it didn't take long for Miles to learn a hard lesson.

The match had hardly gotten going when Aly picked up a bad pass and burst toward the Pride goal.

Miles was right there. He fronted Aly, stayed square, and didn't take any chances.

Aly slowed—as though he had met his match.

Miles moved in a little tighter. Aly looked around, as though he wanted to pass off.

And then Aly made a big mistake—or seemed to.

He let the ball roll off his toe, as though it had slipped away from him.

Miles saw his chance and jumped in. He stroked at the ball.

But the ball was gone!

Aly had swept it away. Miles was left off balance, reaching for the ball.

And now the ball was not only gone, but so was Aly.

Billy came over to help, and so did Tanya, but Aly turned sideways and slipped between them. At the same time, he flipped the ball over his left foot with his right.

Then he picked up the ball with his left foot, stepped, and lashed with his right . . . over the top of the ball.

Nate took the fake and dove to his left. Aly caught his balance and drove the ball right where Nate had been standing.

Heidi saw the ball catch the net, but she still couldn't believe her eyes.

The score was 1 to 0—already.

Aly jumped in the air and shouted something in French. Most of his teammates came over to slap hands with him.

But Heidi noticed something strange.

Jackson and Metzger yelled, "Way to go," or something of that sort. But they didn't seem excited. And they didn't run over to slap hands.

Metzger had been a forward before this season. He was playing midfield now. And Jackson had always been the star. Now he was second best.

As Heidi walked back for the kickoff, she said to Jacob, "Did you see Jackson and Metzger? They don't look so happy about Aly getting all the goals these days."

"They're probably jealous," Jacob said.

"What idiots," Heidi said. "Why would they let something like that bother them?"

She grinned, showing her big dimples.

"I can't think of any reasons. Can you?"

"Not me. It's stupid. They should be happy they have a player that good."

Jacob nodded, but now he looked serious. "I just hope we can stop the guy somehow."

Miles was not far away. Heidi heard him yell to Sterling, "Don't worry. The guy is good. But I won't let him fake me like that again."

Heidi hoped not.

Coach Toscano was yelling for the other fullbacks to double on Aly when he got the ball.

Maybe that would help.

But Heidi also knew that the Pride couldn't think only of defense. They had to get the ball moving.

And for a while neither team got anywhere near the goal.

Miles had made up his mind to stay tough on Aly. And he was doing it.

The other fullbacks were helping out.

The Springers were tough on defense, though, and they were covering Sterling well.

Sterling was good, but he didn't have the dribbling skill—or all the moves—that Aly had.

The match was becoming a stand-off. Minutes kept running off the clock and no one was even threatening to score.

And then Metzger made a move.

He drove up the middle of the field and slipped a pass over to Aly. The defense collapsed on Aly. But Metzger kept right on running.

Aly poked the ball back to him, and Metzger was suddenly in the open.

He came straight at Nate. Adam charged in from the side and cut off Metzger's straight path.

Metzger could have dropped the ball back to Aly, who had cut in his direction.

But Metzger seemed to want this one for himself. He stopped, suddenly, trying to shake Adam loose.

Adam fell back half a step. But then he stepped forward just as Metzger tried to get a shot off.

Adam managed to get a leg in the way and block the shot.

The ball bounced back upfield.

That's when Miles dashed in and trapped the ball. "Attack!" Nate yelled, and the Angel Park players took off.

Miles blasted a long pass upfield, and Jacob ran the ball down. He quickly punched it ahead to Sterling.

The two charged down the middle of the field.

Heidi also ran hard, but she stayed on the wing.

She watched Sterling shoot the ball back over to Jacob. Aly was with them, but he was caught in between. And he had no help from his teammates.

Sterling was moving a little too fast, however. When Aly went after Jacob, Jacob was forced to wait. He couldn't pass to Sterling without getting an offside call.

But Heidi, who was near the touchline, suddenly changed angles and rushed toward Jacob.

She shouted to Jacob, who was fighting to keep control of the ball. Aly was all over him.

Jacob pushed the ball toward Heidi, but he didn't get much power on the pass. By the time she got to it, Aly was on her.

She had to slow and turn to get her body between Aly and the ball.

The other defenders would be catching up quickly. She had to make something happen right now.

She lunged to her right, faking a move, and then she spun around, facing Aly. Aly had taken the fake just enough to throw him a little to one side.

Heidi stepped over the ball, so it was sitting between her feet.

In the instant that Aly's weight was swinging back to his left, Heidi turned, as though she were going to break to her own left.

But she brought her right foot in front of the ball and used her heel to push the ball backward, behind her.

Then she spun around and tapped the ball past Aly. She caught him leaning the wrong way again. That gave her time to make a break past him.

She saw Sterling take off toward the goal. She slipped him a quick pass.

Sterling ran straight at the goalie and then blasted a hard shot at the right corner of the goal.

The ball was heading straight at the goalpost. Heidi thought the shot would hit the post and bounce away.

But it caught the inside of the post and glanced into the net.

For a *score!*

Sterling had tied the match up, 1 to 1.

Heidi ran to him and jumped high to slam hands.

"Great shot!" she shouted.

"Hey, you're the one who did it. What a *move* you put on that guy."

And about then, Aly put his hand on her shoulder. She turned and looked at him.

"You are good," he said. "Very, very good."

"Thanks," Heidi said. She wasn't used to anyone being so polite. "Thanks a lot."

And it was nice to feel good about a goal she hadn't scored.

But the match had a long way to go, and the score was only tied. The Pride still had some serious playing to do.

★ 9 ★

Flying High

The half ended with the score still tied, 1 to 1. The coach told the Pride players they were looking good. They just had to keep going hard and not let down.

"Coach," Heidi said, "I don't think Jackson and Metzger want to pass to Aly. It's like they're jealous of him or something."

"I've noticed that too," the coach said. "But when crunch time comes, those guys will want to win. They'll start going to him."

Heidi glanced at Nate. "Can you believe those guys? How could a player be jealous of his *own* teammate?" She smiled.

"It's hard to believe," he said. And he smiled too.

The coach was talking to Miles now. "Are you getting tired, trying to stay with Aly?" he asked.

"No way. The guy is not scoring on me again. And that's a promise."

It was a great promise. But it only lasted about three minutes into the second half.

Maybe Aly didn't exactly score on Miles. He just happened to be in the right place at the right time.

Jackson took a long shot that had no chance of getting in the goal. Nate was in position, just waiting for the ball to fly into his arms.

But Daniel came over to help out.

He jumped up and blocked the ball off his chest. But he sent it rolling straight at Aly.

Aly took the ball in stride and *zinged* it past Nate and into the net.

The Springers were ahead again, 2 to 1.

Heidi dropped right on the ground when she saw the shot go in. The Angel Park team was right back where it had been—needing two goals to win.

And goals were tough to get against these guys.

The Springer defense tightened all the more now. The Blue Springs kids knew they had the match if they could just keep the Pride from scoring.

There was still plenty of time, but the Springers were playing back. The Pride couldn't seem to find a hole in the defense.

The minutes kept flowing away.

Heidi played hard, working to get open. She tried to center the ball from the wing. Or other times, she charged to the goal herself.

But the Springers were swarming everywhere.

And time kept ticking away.

"Three minutes to go!" Billy shouted from the sidelines. Heidi told herself it was now or never.

She was tired, but so was the fullback who was trying to mark her.

She saw Lian take the ball from a Springer midfielder. She did a quick spin and then *shot* away from her defender.

She got to open space, running toward Lian.

He kicked the ball her way.

She ran to the ball, slowed, controlled it, and spun. Then she darted with the ball back toward the left wing.

The Springers' sweeper tried to cut her off. Heidi stepped over the ball and reversed her direction. Then she darted back toward the center of the field.

She was angling nearer to the goal area. She thought she saw an opening for a shot.

But another fullback came at her from the right. The sweeper was still covering her left side.

She was working her way into a trap.

So she pulled up and suddenly kicked under the ball, lifting it toward the goal.

Sterling and Jacob both broke to the ball. And so did their defenders.

But it was Sterling who took flight like a rocket blasting off.

His head was above everyone, and he caught the ball just right.

He *drove* it at the goal.

But the goalie was in the right spot. He got a hand on the ball and knocked it away.

The ball looped to the left of the goal.

Heidi dashed after it. A Springer defender ran hard for it too.

Heidi got to the ball at about the same time. The two crashed and went down. Another fullback jumped over them and trapped the ball.

But Heidi was up and on the guy before he could clear the ball. Her left foot lashed out and knocked the ball off the guy's shins.

She darted back to the ball and trapped it, but both fullbacks were on her again.

This time she got off a quick pass, right between the two.

Jacob was slicing to the goal. He took the ball out of the air with the inside of his knee.

He dropped the ball to the grass just as the goalie charged.

"Behind you!" Heidi yelled. She had slipped between the fullbacks and was a step ahead of them.

Jacob turned and rolled a little pass her way.

Heidi *exploded* past Jacob and the goalie and slammed the ball into the open net.

Goal!

She had tied the score, 2 to 2.

And the Pride players were all flying high—jumping on each other, screaming, mobbing Heidi.

Jacob grabbed her. "Heidi, you were *everywhere*," he said. "I've never seen you play like that."

"Let's just get another one," she said. "We can still win."

But Aly didn't think so, and neither did Jackson or Metzger.

Both teams played wildly, going all out to get the goal that would give them the championship. But no one could score.

The match ended in a tie.

The referee was quick to shout, "Tie match. We play a five-minute overtime period. You'll have two minutes to get ready, and then we kick off."

All the players walked to the sidelines. Coach Toscano grabbed Heidi and gave her a big hug. "Great job, Heidi," he said. "You've stepped your game up to a whole new level. No one can stay with you when you're playing like that."

"Let's hope so," Heidi said. "We need to score one in this overtime."

"We'll do it!" Henry yelled.

All the other kids cheered.

Heidi really believed no one *could* stop them.

But when she walked back to the field, Heidi could also see that the Springers felt the same way about themselves.

Especially Robbie Jackson.

Soon after the kickoff, Jackson took a pass from Metzger.

Aly made a great break and got open, but Jackson didn't pass to him. He dribbled straight down the field.

He finally got stopped, so he kicked a pass out to his wing. But then he ran hard and called for the ball back. When he got the ball this time, he ran all out, heading for the goal.

And Miles made a mistake. He dropped off Aly and went over to help Adam.

Aly pulled up near the front of the goal area—wide open. He called for the ball.

All Jackson had to do was knock the ball over to him.

But Jackson was driving for his own goal. And he ended up caught in a crowd.

Someone knocked the ball away, and Nate pounced on it.

As the Springers started falling back, Heidi saw Aly shaking his head. Jackson wouldn't even look at him.

Nate set the ball down. He backed off and looked up the field. Then he ran forward and drove a long, low kick up the field.

Henry cut to the ball and trapped it against his middle. Then he booted a pass back to Miles, who was coming up behind him.

Miles nudged a pass off to Heidi on the left.

Heidi broke past her defender and dribbled down the touchline until she saw Lian coming her way. She kicked the ball over to him.

She ran with Lian, and he booted the ball back to her. This time she cut toward the middle of the field. That's when she saw

Henry running a step ahead of his defender, angling to the goal.

She centered a long pass toward him.

Henry was running hard, but the goalie charged the ball too.

Both went up, and for a moment it seemed the goalie would catch the ball. But Henry hit the ball with his head at the same instant the goalie got his hands on it.

The ball bounced away.

At least six players raced toward it—from all angles.

It was Sterling, with his speed, who got there first. But he was in a crowd. He kicked at the ball, and it glanced off someone's legs and rolled free.

Heidi was there.

The goalie had rushed back to the goal, but Heidi had a shot.

She pulled back to fire.

But she saw Henry twisting away from his man and heading for the goal. She rolled a little pass to him.

And Henry fired the ball home!

Rip!

The ball zipped into the net, and the Pride had the lead, 3 to 2.

And *no one* was going to take it away.

The Springers played hard the rest of the way. But they didn't play together. Jackson and Metzger kept trying to get the job done alone. And even Aly seemed to think he had to do it by himself.

That made the defense a lot easier.

The Pride held on and got the victory.

And they celebrated. They jumped all over each other. For a few minutes, everyone went crazy.

And then the players staggered to the side of the field and most of them dropped to the grass. They were completely wiped out.

"How sweet it is!" Billy said. "We did it. We won the championship."

Heidi was lying flat on her back. She turned her head to the side and looked at Nate. *"Champs again!"* she said, hardly believing herself.

"We're getting better all the time, too," Nate said.

"Yeah, and I know why."

Jacob was sitting nearby. "Why?" he asked.

"The dumb coach has had me playing striker when I'm a natural wing. I can't believe it took him so long to figure that out."

"Yeah. He's not as smart as you are," Nate said.

About then, Heidi suddenly got hoisted to her feet. Her dad had pulled her up so he could hug her. Then her mom took a turn.

After that, the coach grabbed her too.

"You were amazing," Coach Toscano said. "Just amazing."

"Hey, *everyone* was," Heidi told him. "Even Nate." She looked down at Nate, who was still on the ground. She grinned. "He used to be a big jerk, but he's not such a bad guy anymore. I helped him overcome his problems."

Nate rolled his eyes. But he was laughing. And then he said one more time, as though he still couldn't believe it, "We did it. We won the championship!"

Final Standings:

Pride	5–1
Springers	4–2
Kickers	4–2
Tornadoes	3–3
Bandits	2–4
Racers	2–4
Gila Monsters	1–5

Match 4 Scores:

Pride	2	Bandits	1
Kickers	4	Gila Monsters	0
Springers	5	Racers	1
Tornadoes	bye		

Match 5 Scores:

Tornadoes	1	Springers	0
Kickers	3	Racers	2
Bandits	2	Gila Monsters	0
Pride	bye		

Match 6 Scores:

Pride	3	Tornadoes	1
Springers	4	Kickers	1
Bandits	2	Racers	0
Gila Monsters	bye		

Match 7 Scores:

Pride	3	Springers	2 (OT)
Racers	4	Gila Monsters	3
Tornadoes	3	Bandits	1
Kickers	bye		

Glossary

corner kick A free kick taken from a corner area by a member of the attacking team, after the defending team has propelled the ball out-of-bounds across the goal line.

cover A defensive maneuver in which a player places himself between an opponent and the goal.

cross pass A pass across the field, often toward the center, intended to set up the shooter.

cutting Suddenly changing directions while dribbling the ball in order to deceive a defender.

direct free kick An unimpeded shot at the goal, awarded to a team sustaining a major foul.

dribbling Maneuvering the ball at close range with only the feet.

feinting Faking out an opponent with deceptive moves.

forwards Players whose primary purpose is to score goals. Also referred to as "strikers."

free kick A direct *or* indirect kick awarded to a team, depending on the type of foul committed by the opposing team.

fullbacks Defensive players whose main purpose is to keep the ball out of the goal area.

goalkeeper The ultimate defender against attacks on the goal, and the only player allowed to use his hands.

halfbacks See Midfielders.

heading Propelling the ball with the head, especially the forehead.

indirect free kick A shot at the goal involving at least two players, awarded to a team sustaining a minor foul.

juggling A drill using the thighs, feet, ankles, or head to keep the ball in the air continuously.

kickoff A center place kick which starts the action at the beginning of both the first and second halves or after a goal has been scored.

marking Guarding a particular opponent.

midfielders Players whose main purpose is to get the ball from the defensive players to the forwards. Also called "halfbacks."

penalty kick A direct free kick awarded to a member of the attacking team from a spot 12 yards in front of the goal. All other players must stay outside the penalty area except for the goalie, who must remain stationary until the ball is in play.

punt   A drop kick made by the goalkeeper.

shooting   Making an attempt to score a goal.

strikers   See Forwards.

sweeper   The last player, besides the goal-keeper, to defend the goal against attack.

tackling   Stealing the ball from an opponent by using the feet or a shoulder charge.

total soccer   A system by which players are constantly shifting positions as the team shifts from offense to defense. Also called "position-less soccer."

volley kick   A kick made while the ball is still in the air.

wall   A defensive barrier of players who stand in front of the goal area to aid the goalkeeper against free kicks.

wall pass   This play involves a short pass from one teammate to another, followed by a return pass to the first player as he runs past the defender. Also called the "give-and-go."

wingbacks   Outside fullbacks.

wingers   Outside forwards.

JOIN THE KIDS FROM ANGEL PARK FOR

#1 KICKOFF TIME
Can a baseball nut like Jacob Scott get the hang of a new sport—or should he just give up and wait for baseball season?

#2 DEFENSE!
It's up to goalie Nate Matheson to lead the Angel Park Pride to victory—but first he's got to learn to stop yelling at his teammates!

#3 VICTORY GOAL
A defensive soccer player, Sterling is sick of letting his teammates get all the glory—until a very special person shows him that sometimes taking risks can be more important than winning…

#4 PSYCHED!
When the Angel Park Pride starts taking the game a little too seriously, fun-loving Heidi comes up with a surefire plan to get the team psyched and ready!

MORE FAST-KICKING SOCCER ACTION!

#5 BACKUP GOALIE

It's up to goalie Nate to save his team's chance for the championship—but how can he do that when he's out with an injury and can't even play?

#6 TOTAL SOCCER

Clayton Lindsay may be the Pride's best player, but if he doesn't stop hogging the ball and work with his teammates, he's going to blow it for everyone!

#7 SHAKE-UP

The Pride players get a quick lesson in what teamwork is all about when an earthquake rocks the Angel Park area.

BULLSEYE BOOKS PUBLISHED BY RANDOM HOUSE, INC.

Read the ANGEL PARK ALL-STARS

#1 Making the Team
Can Kenny, Harlan, and Jacob—the newest rookies on the team—stand up to some big-league bullying?

#2 Big Base Hit
Harlan can't seem to do anything right—until everything comes together for that big base hit!

#3 Winning Streak
Kenny's in a slump, and that means trouble for the Dodgers—until Jacob hits on the one thing that will get Kenny back in action!

#4 What a Catch!
When everything else fails, a pep talk from a major-league pro helps get Brian back on track—and not a minute too soon!

#5 Rookie Star
Sure, Kenny's good. But when he starts acting like a star, the whole team starts fighting. Can the Dodgers get it together before it's too late?

FOR ALL-STAR BASEBALL EXCITEMENT!

#6 PRESSURE PLAY

When their rivals start playing dirty, Jacob uses his brains instead of his bat to put the Dodgers back in the running for the championship.

#7 LINE DRIVE

Lian Jie may be small, but he's got what it takes to be a Dodger—if only the team would give him a chance to prove himself!

#8 CHAMPIONSHIP GAME

Can the Dodgers keep their coach from wrecking their chance at the championship—or is it all over for Angel Park?

BULLSEYE BOOKS PUBLISHED BY RANDOM HOUSE, INC.